SWEET BETSY FROM PIKE

SWEET BETSY FROM PIKE

❧ A SONG FROM THE GOLD RUSH DAYS ☙

ILLUSTRATED BY

Robert Andrew Parker

THE VIKING PRESS   NEW YORK

First Edition
Copyright © Robert Andrew Parker, 1978
All rights reserved
First published in 1978 by The Viking Press
625 Madison Avenue, New York, N. Y. 10022
Published simultaneously in Canada by
Penguin Books Canada Limited
Printed in U.S.A.
1 2 3 4 5 82 81 80 79 78

Library of Congress Cataloging in Publication Data
Main entry under title: Sweet Betsy from Pike.
   Summary: Betsy crosses the plains with Ike
to look for gold in California.
   [1. Folk songs, American] I. Parker, Robert Andrew.
PZ8.3.S9953   [E]   77-13924
ISBN 0-670-68632-8

FOR PETER KANE DUFAULT

Oh, don't you remember Sweet Betsy from Pike,
Who crossed the big mountains with her lover Ike,
With two yoke of cattle, a large yellow dog,
A tall Shanghai rooster, and one spotted hog.

Refrain   Saying, "Good-by, Pike County,
                        Farewell for a while.
                        We'll come back again
                        When we've panned out our pile."

One evening quite early they camped on the Platte.
'Twas nearby the road on a green shady flat,
Where Betsy, quite tired, lay down to repose,
While Ike gazed with wonder on his Pike County rose.

Refrain   Saying, "Good-by, Pike County,
                 Farewell for a while.
                 We'll come back again
                 When we've panned out our pile."

They soon reached the desert, where Betsy gave out,
And down in the sand she lay rolling about,
While Ike in great tears looked on in surprise,
Saying, "Betsy, get up, you'll get sand in your eyes."

Refrain   Saying, "Good-by, Pike County,
                  Farewell for a while.
                  We'll come back again
                  When we've panned out our pile."

Sweet Betsy got up in a great deal of pain
And declared she'd go back to Pike County again.
Then Ike heaved a sigh, and they fondly embraced,
And she traveled along with his arm 'round her waist.

Refrain   Saying, "Good-by, Pike County,
                   Farewell for a while.
                   We'll come back again
                   When we've panned out our pile."

The Shanghai ran off and the cattle all died.
The last piece of bacon that morning was fried.
Poor Ike got discouraged, and Betsy got mad.
The dog wagged his tail and looked wonderfully sad.

Refrain　　　　Saying, "Good-by, Pike County,
　　　　　　　　Farewell for a while.
　　　　　　　　We'll come back again
　　　　　　　　When we've panned out our pile."

They passed the Sierras through mountains of snow
Till old California was sighted below.
Sweet Betsy she hollered, and Ike gave a cheer,
Saying, "Betsy, my darling, I'm a new millionaire."

Refrain   Saying, "Good-by, Pike County,
                    Farewell for a while.
                    We'll come back again
                    When we've panned out our pile."

One morning they climbed up a very high hill
And looked down with wonder at old Placerville;
Ike shouted and said when he cast his eyes down,
"Sweet Betsy, my darling, there's gold in this town!"

Refrain   Saying, "Good-by, Pike County,
                     Farewell for a while.
                     We'll come back again
                     When we've panned out our pile."

Long Ike and Sweet Betsy attended a dance,
Where Ike wore a pair of his Pike County pants.
Sweet Betsy was covered with ribbons and rings.
Ike said, "You're an angel, but where are your wings?"

Refrain   Saying, "Good-by, Pike County,
Farewell for a while.
We'll come back again
When we've panned out our pile."

A miner said, "Betsy, will you dance with me?"
"I will, old hoss, if you don't make too free.
But don't dance me hard. Do you want to know why?
Doggone ye, I'm chock-full of strong alkali."

Refrain   Saying, "Good-by, Pike County,
                Farewell for a while.
                We'll come back again
                When we've panned out our pile."

Long Ike and Sweet Betsy got married, of course,
But Ike became jealous and got a divorce.
While Betsy, well satisfied, said with a shout,
"Good-by, you big lummox, I'm glad you backed out."

Refrain   Saying, "Good-by, dear Isaac,
Farewell for a while.
But come back in time
To replenish my pile."

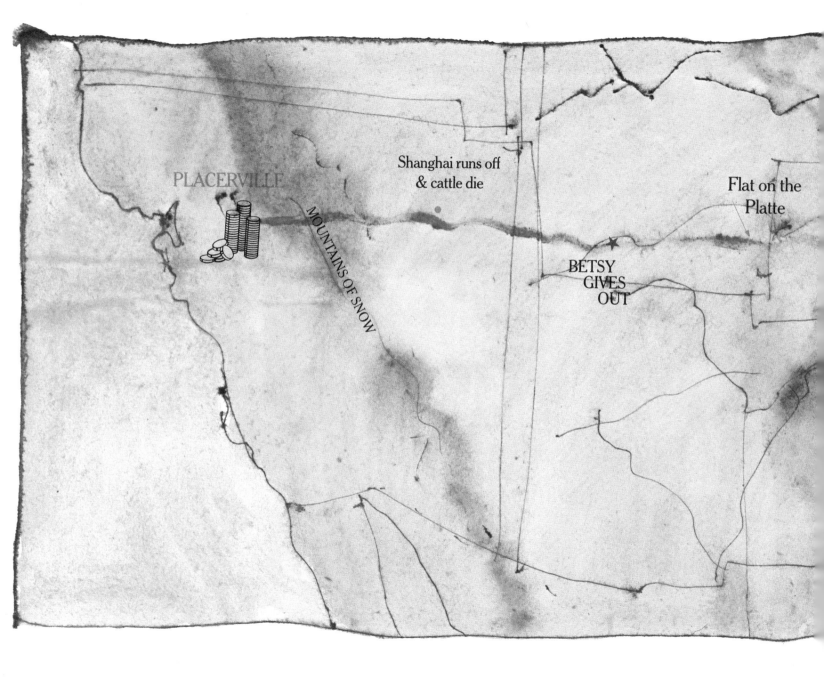

PLACERVILLE

Shanghai runs off
& cattle die

Flat on the
Platte

MOUNTAINS OF SNOW

BETSY
GIVES
OUT

"GOOD-BY, PIKE COUNTY"

PIKE COUNTY
Missouri

SWEET BETSY and LONG IKE'S ROUTE
MAP

SWEET BETSY FROM PIKE

Oh, don't you re-mem-ber Sweet Bet-sy from Pike, Who crossed the big
mount-ains with her lov-er Ike, With two yoke of cat-tle, a
large yel-low dog, A tall Shang-hai roost-er, and one spot-ted

REFRAIN

hog. Say-ing, "Good-by, Pike Coun-ty, Fare-well for a while.
We'll come back a-gain When we've panned out our pile."

2. One evening quite early they camped on the Platte.
'Twas nearby the road on a green shady flat,
Where Betsy, quite tired, lay down to repose,
While Ike gazed with wonder on his Pike County rose.

3. They soon reached the desert, where Betsy gave out,
And down in the sand she lay rolling about,
While Ike in great tears looked on in surprise,
Saying, "Betsy, get up, you'll get sand in your eyes."

4. Sweet Betsy got up in a great deal of pain
And declared she'd go back to Pike County again.
Then Ike heaved a sigh, and they fondly embraced,
And she traveled along with his arm 'round her waist.

5. The Shanghai ran off and the cattle all died.
The last piece of bacon that morning was fried.
Poor Ike got discouraged, and Betsy got mad.
The dog wagged his tail and looked wonderfully sad.

6. They passed the Sierras through mountains of snow
   Till old California was sighted below.
   Sweet Betsy she hollered, and Ike gave a cheer,
   Saying, "Betsy, my darling, I'm a new millionaire."

7. One morning they climbed up a very high hill
   And looked down with wonder at old Placerville;
   Ike shouted and said when he cast his eyes down,
   "Sweet Betsy, my darling, there's gold in this town!"

8. Long Ike and Sweet Betsy attended a dance,
   Where Ike wore a pair of his Pike County pants.
   Sweet Betsy was covered with ribbons and rings.
   Ike said, "You're an angel, but where are your wings?"

9. A miner said, "Betsy, will you dance with me?"
   "I will, old hoss, if you don't make too free.
   But don't dance me hard. Do you want to know why?
   Doggone ye, I'm chock-full of strong alkali."

10. Long Ike and Sweet Betsy got married, of course,
    But Ike became jealous and got a divorce.
    While Betsy, well satisfied, said with a shout,
    "Good-by, you big lummox, I'm glad you backed out."

Refrain   Saying, "Good-by, dear Isaac,
             Farewell for a while.
             But come back in time
             To replenish my pile."

About the Illustrator

Robert Andrew Parker was graduated from the Art Institute of Chicago. He has illustrated numerous children's books and has long been recognized as one of America's outstanding painters. His work is represented in leading museum collections, including the Museum of Modern Art, the Whitney Museum of American Art, the Morgan Library in New York, and in private collections. He lives in Washington, Connecticut, with his family.

About This Book

The text type used in *Sweet Betsy from Pike* is Linotype Granjon, and the display type faces are Cowpoke and Playbill. The art work was done with acrylic used as gouache, watercolor, and pen and ink; it was camera preseparated. Printed by offset, the book is bound in cloth over boards and is side-sewn.